MICHAEL DAHL'S
REALLY SCARY STORIES

Raintree is an imprint of Capstone Global Library Limited, a company
incorporated in England and Wales having its registered office at
264 Banbury Road, Oxford, OX2 7DY — Registered company number: 6695582

www.raintree.co.uk
myorders@raintree.co.uk

Edited by Eliza Leahy
Designed by Tracy McCabe
Original illustrations © Capstone 2017
Illustrated by Xavier Bonet
Image Credits: Shutterstock: Dmitry Natashin, black box design element
Production by Kathy McColley
Printed and bound in China.

ISBN 978 1 4747 4417 1
21 20 19 18 17
10 9 8 7 6 5 4 3 2 1

British Library Cataloguing in Publication Data
A full catalogue record for this book is available from the British Library.

Acknowledgements
Every effort has been made to contact copyright holders of material
reproduced in this book. Any omissions will be rectified in subsequent
printings if notice is given to the publisher.

THE NIGHT
OCTOPUS
AND OTHER SCARY TALES

CONTENTS

But as Tina watched in horror, she saw a skinny white arm reach over the edge of the bridge and grab the rear tyre of Nyssa's bike.

The men grew thinner before his eyes. Their backs arched and their shoulders hunched over. Their hair whitened and fell out in clumps onto the ground.

In the darkness, something growled as hot breath tickled the back of Min's neck. From below, at the bottom of the steps, came more growls.

Dear Reader,

When I was a child, there was a deep ravine that divided my neighbourhood.

One summer morning, my friend Ricky and I descended the ravine on the way to visit our friend Phillip.

Ricky suddenly stopped and put his finger to his lips. A weak voice was floating up from the bottom of the ravine: "Help . . ." We both heard it.

We ran to a nearby petrol station and told the men working there. They followed us to the ravine. Soon we all heard, "Help . . . help . . ."

Then we saw it. A white kitten emerged from behind a dead tree. It meowed softly, sounding exactly like a child crying for help.

Not everything sounds – or looks – as it seems.

So if you hear strange noises or voices while you read the following stories, just ignore them. And if you feel something furry crawling into your bed late at night, just tell yourself it's a friendly kitten.

I'M SURE IT'S NOTHING TO WORRY ABOUT . . .

THE DARKEST BRIDGE

It was midnight when the three bikes stopped in the middle of a bridge. The bridge spanned a deep ravine. Far below, a swiftly moving stream was quietly murmuring.

"What's wrong?" said Tina. "Why did you stop?"

Her older sister, Zoe, her hands still on the handlebars of her bike, looked at her and smiled. "Don't you know where we are?"

"I do," piped up a voice behind them. It was Tina's friend Nyssa. "It's the haunted bridge."

"Are you kidding me?" said Tina.

"It's true," said Nyssa. "Right, Zoe?"

The girls had gone to see a scary movie in town

that night. On the way home, Zoe had decided to lead them on a different route. They had ridden away from the lights of the small town towards a thick forest. After riding down a country road lined with tall trees, they reached the old wooden bridge.

"Are you telling me there are ghosts living on the bridge?" asked Tina.

Tina loved scary movies. She also loved watching TV shows about ghost hunters and listening to podcasts about weird and spooky events in history. She had never actually seen a ghost herself, but she hoped to.

"Not *on* the bridge," said Nyssa. "*Under* the bridge."

"That's not exactly the story," said Zoe.

"Tell me!" begged Tina. She had to know.

Zoe turned so she could see both girls. "It was eighty years ago tonight," she began. "Some children were coming back from a church picnic."

"A picnic at night?" asked Tina.

"It was all day," said Zoe. "They had a bonfire or something at night. Anyway, these children were riding their bikes back to town. It started raining, and they were crossing this very bridge –"

Tina heard a sound somewhere on the other side of the bridge. An owl?

"The girl whose bike was the last one over the bridge hit a patch of water," continued Zoe.

"That doesn't sound good," said Tina. The owl hooted again.

Zoe said, "Her bike skidded. She plunged down the ravine until she landed in the creek at the bottom!"

"Poor girl," said Nyssa.

Zoe nodded. She wheeled her bike to the edge of the bridge and looked down. The other two followed her. They all gazed into the blackness below.

"So what happened?" asked Tina. "Does she haunt the bridge? Will we see her walking around?"

"Will we hear her scream?" whispered Nyssa.

Zoe shook her head. "It's spookier than that. They say that sometimes . . . sometimes, if you're riding your bike over this bridge, it will stop and you won't be able to move."

"Why?" asked Tina.

"The dead girl needs another bike to ride home," said Zoe. "So she'll grab yours because hers is down in the water."

"That *is* spookier," agreed Nyssa.

"Wait!" cried Tina. "I can't move my bike! She's grabbed it!"

The other girls laughed.

"What's so funny?" said Tina. The fear made her angry.

"Zoe," said Nyssa, giggling. "She's holding the back of your bike!"

Zoe laughed out loud.

"Very funny," muttered Tina. "Let's get out of here."

"Wait!" said Nyssa. "What's that?"

They heard a faint bump. Then another. It came from behind them, towards the end of the bridge. One after another, the wooden planks creaked. It sounded as though a bike was riding onto the bridge.

"You're doing that!" Tina shouted at Zoe.

"No, I'm not," said her sister.

"I'm getting out of here," Tina said.

She mounted her bike and pushed the pedals as fast as she could. Zoe was close behind her.

Nyssa shouted. "I can't move!" she said. "My wheels are locked or something. I'm not making it up. Help me!"

"I don't believe you," yelled Tina.

"Please!" begged Nyssa.

There were no lights on the bridge. Only their dim bike headlights lit the surroundings. But as Tina watched in horror, she saw a skinny white arm reach over the edge of the bridge and grab the rear tyre of Nyssa's bike.

Suddenly, the three headlights flickered and went out. The girls were now in a thick darkness.

"She's got my foot!" screamed Nyssa.

Tina jumped off her bike, pushed it aside and

ran onto the darkened bridge. She felt for the nearest railing and followed it to where she had last seen her friend.

"Don't go!" shouted Zoe.

Tina walked further and further onto the bridge. She waved her free hand around, hoping to touch Nyssa or her bike. "Nyssa, where are you?" she called.

There was no sound except for the murmur of the stream below. Then the murmur grew louder. It became a loud hum and then a rumble.

"Nyssa!" shouted Tina desperately. "Where are you?"

The rumble grew even louder, and then a flash of light. Two lights. A huge truck was racing down the road. It roared onto the bridge.

Tina felt a small hand gripping her ankle as the lights grew brighter than the sun and smashed through the darkness. The small hand gave a sharp yank. A wave of cold air surrounded Tina as she toppled off the bridge. The truck rumbled overhead. Tina fell through the darkness. She heard Nyssa's screams from far below as she plunged down to join her.

THE WAITING POOL

Grant was warm, but he wasn't sweating nearly as much as his father. "Ready for our new pool?" asked Mr Costello.

Grant rolled his eyes. "Dad, it's a paddling pool."

"A super-fancy paddling pool," said Mr Costello. He and Grant stood in their backyard. The sun blazed down on them from a cloudless, blue sky. The big, blue paddling pool had taken Mr Costello two hours to put together. It was four metres wide and surrounded by a plastic wall 60 cm high. A small set of plastic steps helped would-be paddlers climb over the edge.

"I couldn't believe it was free," said Mr Costello. "The guy at the garage sale knocked it down to five bucks. I still wasn't sure if I should buy it. Then he comes up and whispers, 'It's yours. I don't want it anymore!' Boom."

Grant put his hand on the stiff plastic wall. "Is it OK?" he asked. "I mean, if it's OK, why did the guy get rid of it?"

Mr Costello shrugged. "Maybe his kids got too big for it," he said. "Maybe he wanted to put in a real pool. Who knows? But you can't argue with free."

Grant pulled his hand away from the pool wall.

"What's wrong?" asked his dad.

"I don't know," said Grant, gazing at his hand. "It felt like . . ."

"It's hot from sitting out in this crazy sun. Come on, let's fill this baby up," said Mr Costello. He walked over to the house and picked up the end of a long garden hose. Twenty minutes later, the pool was full.

"Let it warm up," said his father. "Water straight from the hose is cold."

When Mr Costello went inside to cool off, Grant stayed out in the yard and played Frisbee with his dog, Gump. Suddenly, Gump started barking. Grant turned and saw an old man leaning over the pool.

His stringy white hair fell past his shoulders. His skin was wrinkled like a crumpled-up piece of paper. His fingernails were long and yellow.

The man kept staring into the pool. Gump barked a few more times, and the man turned. He blinked his watery grey eyes at Grant a few times. Then a weird look came over his face. He coughed and spat and muttered words that Grant couldn't understand. He waved his arms wildly over his head and then stumbled in Grant's direction.

Grant ran towards the house, Gump running alongside and barking.

The boy reached the screen door and rushed inside. Quickly, he locked the handle. He gazed through the screen and shouted, "Go away!" But the man was gone.

He waited a few minutes to make sure the man didn't come back. Then Grant opened the door, and he and Gump stepped outside. The backyard was empty. The pool sat quietly, reflecting the blazing sun.

The boy walked over to where the ancient man had been standing. He stared into the pool. The water lapped gently back and forth against the curving plastic wall. Grant thought something must have disturbed its surface. But there was nothing there in the clear water.

Had the hot sun made him see things? If so, why had Gump barked? The dog couldn't be seeing things, too.

* * *

Grant avoided the pool for the rest of the day. But the next afternoon, two of his friends came over to check it out.

The boys splashed and played in the water, throwing a ball back and forth. Even Gump jumped into the pool a few times. Eventually Grant forgot all about the strange man from the day before.

"It's pretty cool for a little kid's pool," said Grant's friend Li.

"Yeah, it's awesome," agreed his friend Rodey.

Suddenly Li got a frightened look on his face. He pointed to the middle of the pool.

"What's that?" he shouted.

The boys stood against the curving plastic wall as the water in the middle bubbled and churned.

A hand rose out of the water. Li screamed. The hand was followed by a bony shoulder and then a head, covered in long, wet, stringy hair. It was the old man. The other boys screamed. The old man reached out to them, grasping at their legs and feet. Grant felt hard fingers trying to hold onto his right foot, but he kicked them away.

The boys climbed out of the pool as quickly as they could, tumbling onto the grass and scrambling to their feet. From a safe distance, they stood barefoot in the grass. Grant watched the old man disappear underwater.

"Get away from there!" Rodey yelled to Grant.

Grant looked over at his friends, who had run towards the house. Instead of his friends, there stood two old men.

The men grew thinner before his eyes. Their backs arched and their shoulders hunched. Their hair whitened and fell out in clumps. Their arms and bare legs grew thin and frail. Wrinkles spread across their faces like the webs of spiders. One of the men opened his mouth to speak and a tooth fell out.

"What's going on?" said Grant. "Who are you?"

The old men wore the same swimming trunks and T-shirts as Li and Rodey. They tried answering Grant, but weird sounds came from their mouths. They couldn't speak. They could only mumble.

Grant looked quickly at the pool. Where had that old man gone?

Grant decided he was going to ask the old men what they had done to his friends, but his mouth wasn't working properly. His tongue was thick, and his lips were numb. He raised a hand to feel his face, but the hand he saw was not his hand. It couldn't be. It was pale and flabby. The fingernails were sharp and yellow.

The back door of the house banged open. Grant's father stood there. "What are you doing in my yard?" he yelled. "Get out of here," he said, "or I'll call the police!"

"Dad! It's me," shouted Grant. But the words didn't come out that way. His voice sounded more like a growl.

"Get out, I said," shouted Mr Costello. "Or so help me." He took a threatening step towards the men.

The two old men fled across the yard.

Grant stood there a moment longer. He saw an old dog panting at his father's feet. The dog reminded him of a dog he had owned a long time ago. What was its name again? Gumbo? Grump?

While Grant watched, the dog crumbled to the ground. Its body turned to dust and its grey hair floated off in the breeze. His father looked down at the powder that had once been their dog and cried out.

Mr Costello covered his face with his hands. Then he stared at the old man who had not run away. "Do I know you?" he asked.

Grant tried to speak, but more of his teeth fell out.

"You look familiar," said Mr Costello. He had a sad, confused look on his face. The man glanced around the yard. "Where's my son? What have you done with Grant?"

Grant's vision blurred. He could barely hear his

father's voice. He forgot where he was. *Whose house is this?* he wondered. A single image stayed in his memory. *The water,* he thought. *I must reach the water!*

Grant turned slowly and limped towards the swimming pool. Every step seemed to last a year.

The sun burned hotter against his ageing flesh. The sweat poured down his body. As the sweat dripped, it pulled pieces of his skin along with it. The bones underneath gleamed in the blazing sunlight.

Grant was less than a metre away from the pool when the breeze grew stronger and the white bones crumbled to dust.

BIG
FURRY

"Min! Run downstairs and grab me a jar of peaches," said her mum, who was laying plates and silverware on the table for dinner.

Min bit her lower lip and didn't move.

Her mum set down the stack of plates and put a hand on the back of a chair. "Did you hear what I said?" she asked.

"Why can't Tray get them?" said Min.

"Because I asked you, young lady," her mum replied.

Min walked into the kitchen and shot a quick glance at the cellar door. Her hands began to shake a little.

Tray ran into the kitchen right behind his older sister. "Min's afraid of the dark," he chanted. "Min's afraid of the dark."

Isn't everyone afraid of the dark? thought Min.

Her mum brushed past them and hurried over to check her pans on the hob. "Now hurry up, Min. Dinner will be ready soon."

Min took a few careful steps towards the cellar door.

Her mum hurried back into the dining room. "Tray, go and wash your face," she called over her shoulder. "I have to get dressed before your father gets here."

"Min's not going downstairs!" called Tray, blocking the doorway between the kitchen and dining room.

"MIN!" came her mum's voice.

Min scowled at her brother. She walked over to the cellar door and angrily yanked it open.

"See?" she said. "Does it look like I'm afraid?"

Tray said nothing. His smile vanished as he stared at the open door.

He's afraid of going downstairs too, Min told herself.

Old wooden stairs led straight down, stopped at a small landing, twisted to the right, and then slid into darkness. On the left-hand wall was a set of hooks to hang their winter coats, scarves and hats. A small wooden box near the door held their gloves and mittens.

Min never minded opening the cellar door to grab her coat and scarf. But the thought of walking down those stairs made her shiver. Especially as it was always cold down there. Now, with winter on its way, the cold air from the cellar swirled around her bare legs as soon as she opened the door.

"Go on, Min," said her brother.

"Be quiet," she snapped. Min slowly stepped through the doorway and started down the stairs.

BANG!

Min was swallowed up in blackness. The door had slammed shut. She felt for the door handle and pushed it. It wouldn't budge. She could hear her brother giggling on the other side.

"Tray!" called Min. "Open the door!"

Tray giggled again. "I have to go and wash my face," he said. Min heard his footsteps racing away, growing softer.

"Tray!" she yelled again. Min pounded on the door. Her mum was getting dressed. Her father wasn't home yet.

Min shivered. The cold air crept up her legs. It climbed up her arms and neck.

I'm not going downstairs, Min told herself. She decided to stay where she was. She would just wait until she heard her mum return to the kitchen. *Then Tray will get it,* she thought, smiling.

Min rubbed her arms. The air was freezing. Her back bumped against the wall, and she felt something big and furry drop onto her shoulders. The girl jumped. She relaxed as she saw, in the dim light squeezing under the door, that it was only a coat. *Mum's winter coat,* thought Min. *Perfect.* As long as she had to wait, she decided she should at least be comfortable.

In the darkness, Min pulled the big coat tighter. The fur felt so nice and warm. Along with the warmth, she felt something else. A slight vibration . . . like a beating heart. Min felt two long, hairy arms reach out from the back and wrap themselves around her. Something growled as hot breath tickled the back of Min's neck. From below, at the bottom of the steps, came more growls. What looked like a forest of shaggy lumps with long, black tongues and furry arms, topped by tiny blazing eyes, came lumbering up the stairs.

A HAND IN THE DARK

Jasmine ran down the blue, glowing corridor, her ticket stub in one hand and a bucket of popcorn in the other. The ticket manager, a young guy with a smirk, had told Jasmine "her boyfriend" was waiting for her.

Boyfriend? Angus was just a good friend. A partner in crime. It had been Angus's idea to go to see the silly monster movie instead of working on their world history project that Saturday morning.

As she ran down the dim corridor, she passed a poster for the movie they were planning to see – *Absorbo*. A blobby monster made of goo that could change shape and eat people. Talk about pathetic!

Jasmine spotted Angus leaning against the wall

outside the cinema. He was chewing on a licorice stick. "Sorry I'm late," said Jasmine.

Angus shrugged as if to say, "No big deal." He gestured towards the door and they both made their way into the dark cinema.

No one else was there. *Perfect,* thought Jasmine. It would be cool to have an entire cinema screen to themselves.

After several previews, the movie finally started.

"Where did you hear about this movie?" asked Jasmine.

"Online somewhere," Angus mumbled. "Should be fun."

"I promise I won't scream at the scary parts," Jasmine said.

"Me too," Angus said with a grin.

Jasmine thought of that promise after only ten minutes. The monster looked horrible. It was a mass of some weird jelly-like substance made by a mad scientist. And after it killed the scientist, it took his shape. Then it started attacking people who worked with him. It always killed its victims by absorbing their bodies into its gooey body.

Disgusting!

When the monster lunged towards its next victim, Jasmine let out a scream. She hadn't meant to. Angus only grunted. But what was worse, she'd grabbed onto Angus's hand. Totally embarrassing.

But Angus hadn't let go. Hmm . . . was he her boyfriend after all?

"I'm glad you picked this movie," said Jasmine.

"The monster is so stupid, right?" he said.

Jasmine giggled. "They see the monster on the other side of the room and they still don't run away," she said. "They just stand there."

Another boy walked into the cinema, holding a bucket of popcorn. *So we won't have the screen all to ourselves,* thought Jasmine. *Oh well.*

"Oh, you've already got popcorn," said the new boy.

Jasmine looked at him, standing in the shadows. Was he talking to them? How rude. As he stepped towards the light from the screen, Jasmine could see his face. It was Angus. "Jasmine," said the new arrival, "I'm sorry I'm so late, but –" The boy froze.

He wasn't looking at Jasmine. He was looking past her. His face grew pale and he dropped his bucket of popcorn, kernels falling all over his jeans and shoes.

"What?" asked Jasmine. Angus was still holding her hand. But his hand had suddenly turned cold and wet.

She was afraid to turn and look at Angus, the one sitting next to her. She was afraid of what she might see.

"Jasmine!" screamed the standing boy.

The girl felt the hand she was holding onto grow wider, fatter, gooier. It seemed to slide up her arm and began absorbing her into its dark, jelly-like mass.

FLUSHED

The water swirled rapidly down the toilet with a loud gurgle. "Where do all the goldfish go?" asked Rachel.

"Down," said her older sister, Pamela.

The two young girls stood over the toilet in their bathroom. They had just flushed another dead goldfish – the seventh or eighth? – into the swirling waters. Its final, fishy resting place.

Rachel peered into the water. "Do you think they'll ever swim back?"

"They're dead," said Pamela. "They're gone. The water flushes them out into the ocean or something."

"What if this time the goldfish wasn't dead?" Rachel worried aloud. "Maybe it was just sleeping. Sleeping looks like dead."

"It was not sleeping. It was ill," said Pamela. She lowered the toilet lid and walked back to their bedroom. Rachel followed close behind.

Pamela flopped down on her bed and picked up a magazine. "Goldfish get ill so easily," she said, flipping the magazine pages.

"But everybody can get poorly," said Rachel.

"Not me," said Pamela. "I don't even get colds."

Rachel sighed. Her throat was feeling scratchy. Her nose was bunged up when she woke that morning too. Rachel hated colds.

"The fish wouldn't have been ill if you hadn't fed it so much," said Pamela, without looking up from her reading.

"But it was hungry," Rachel protested.

"How can you tell?"

"Its sad, sad eyes," said Rachel.

"Fish eyes all look the same," Pamela said.

:l coughed. She put her hand to her throat and rubbed it.

Pamela looked up quickly and stared at her sister.

"What?" demanded Rachel. "What's your problem?"

Pamela's eyes were wide and frightened. "Nothing. Never mind."

Rachel looked away. She did not want to get a cold. Everyone would make too much fuss.

But the next morning, she couldn't get out of bed. Her mother came into the bedroom, sat next to Rachel, and felt her forehead. "Oh dear," said her mother. "It's a fever."

"I don't have a fever," mumbled Rachel from her damp pillow.

"Shh!" whispered her mother.

The woman looked around the room, as if afraid that someone was listening to them. She looked down at her daughter and shook her head. "And you looked flushed too," she said.

"Flushed?" said Rachel quietly.

"Your face is all red, honey," said her mother. "I'll go and get you a cold cloth for your forehead." She bent down close and said, "I'll tell your sister. Don't worry, Rachel. I know you'll get better soon."

Rachel watched her mother walk out of the room. *I don't have a cold,* she thought. *I don't! And Mum is right. I'll feel better soon. It's nothing.*

The next day, she felt worse. Her temperature had risen. Her throat was raw and raspy. Her cough could be heard throughout the house.

Pamela came to see her sister. She stood by the door with a frown on her face. "Can you please keep it down?" she said. "Everyone can hear you."

"I can't help it," said Rachel. Suddenly, she coughed again, long and loud.

Pamela looked up at the ceiling. "Too late," she said.

Outside the house, two huge gold-coloured fins reached down. The fins gripped either side of the building, raised it up in the air, and then began shaking it. Screams and shouts could be heard within.

A moment later, the front door of the house, facing downwards, flipped open. Rachel fell from the door and plunged through the air. She landed in a vast white bowl filled with water. As soon as she hit the surface, the water began to swirl faster and faster, and then gurgled as it disappeared into a huge, dark tunnel.

Gently, the gold fins put the house back down.

A strange voice, high above the house said, "They get ill so often."

"I know," came a second voice. "But there's nothing we can do."

The first speaker smacked its big, blobby lips. "I hate watching them go," it said. "They have such sad, sad eyes."

THE
HORNLOCK

Larry was running down the alley a few blocks away from his house. Except for the frightened boy, the alley was empty.

Whap . . . whap . . .

The pounding of his shoes echoed off the walls of the garages lining his path.

Darkness closed in on him. Larry locked his eyes on the streetlight at the end of the alley. If only he could reach the light before . . .

Before it caught him.

Before it ripped him to shreds with its four massive claws.

He had to reach the light. But the faster Larry

ran, the faster the streetlight seemed to move away from him.

Larry halted to catch his breath, leaning against a garage for support. Goosebumps prickled the back of his neck. The moaning. He could still hear the strange, high-pitched moaning behind him.

It was not the wind that howled. It was the thing. The beast.

The Hornlock.

The creature was a family curse. For years it had hunted them. It began decades earlier when his grandfather had been killed in a strange hunting accident. It was no bear that had attacked him. It was something much worse.

And now the same creature had found Larry.

Larry pushed away from the garage and dashed towards the streetlight. This time the light stood still. It didn't glide further away like before. The lamp's glow grew brighter and brighter.

The howls grew louder. Closer.

Strength was draining from Larry's body. His lungs burned. His chest tightened with a knot of pain. He couldn't feel his feet. Larry had been running for so long, he didn't know what time it was. He only knew that it was late. And dark. He couldn't even remember what day it was.

Another howl ripped through the night. The boy lowered his head, gritted his teeth and strained with all his muscles. He had to reach the end of the alley.

Bang!

The light went out. The boy looked up. The streetlight was blocked by a large shadow. The shadow howled and reached out with four powerful arms. Deadly talons at the ends of the paws shined green with an eerie light.

The boy's shoulders were gripped tightly.

Larry screamed.

"Larry! Larry!" came a voice.

Larry opened his eyes and saw his mother. His bedroom had vanished. Then he remembered he had decided to sleep out on the front porch that night. It was a cool summer night, and the sound of crickets had lulled him to sleep. His mother was sitting on the edge of the air bed he slept on, shaking him awake.

It was just a dream, he thought. A stupid dream about a monster, because he'd been reading horror comics before bed.

"What time is it?" he said.

"It doesn't matter," said his mother. "Now hurry up and get out of bed. We don't have much time."

"What's going on? Where's Dad?"

A man's scream shook the house. Larry threw the covers off and hopped up from the bed. Comics spilled off the sheets. He was wide awake now.

"Larry, don't!" cried his mother. The boy shrugged his mother's hand off his shoulder and ran into the house.

The house was dark, but he could still see from the light of the streetlamps outside filtering through the windows. He turned a corner, heading into the living room. A face jumped into view. His father. He looked shocked. No, he looked terrified!

"The Hornlock, Larry!" said his father. "The Hornlock is in the house!"

And this time, it was not a dream.

THE NIGHT OCTOPUS

Simone stared at the wispy white curtains clawing the air, waving like silent tentacles.

Every time she visited her great-aunt Glory, she stayed in the upstairs back bedroom. It was the biggest room upstairs and had windows on two walls, making it also the brightest room. Sunlight shimmered through those curtains. Moonlight too.

Simone liked the room's old-fashioned wallpaper with its big flowers and hummingbirds. The bed was wide and comfy, covered with plump pillows. A tall blue wardrobe facing the bed had plenty of room for her week's worth of clothes.

"What do you think, Fred?" Simone asked as she

dropped an orange ball of fur onto the bedroom floor. Her new kitten bounced onto the bed. He pawed a few times at the soft pink blanket and started to purr.

"Glad you like it," said Simone.

Aunt Glory insisted that all the windows in the house stay open in the summer. If Simone closed them before she went to bed, she would find them open again in the morning. The old woman made sure the windows were open as she made her nightly rounds. "Fresh air is good for the soul," she would say.

Tonight, Simone wasn't thinking of her soul when she stared at the open windows. Simone didn't like what the breeze did to the curtains.

They moved.

The curtains fluttered without a sound in the light breeze, grasping at the air. The waving fabric reminded her of the arms of an octopus. During a school field trip to the aquarium, Simone and her friends had walked through a dark tunnel enclosed by glass. Sea creatures of all sizes and colours drifted above and beside them. Simone was startled by a large octopus, its long rubbery arms reaching towards her. The suckers stuck to the glass, reminding Simone of ugly little mouths. The octopus's eyes, as large as tennis balls, seemed to stare at her. Its body ballooned with air. Its sticky mouths opened and shut. Frightened, Simone ran down the dark tunnel as the octopus followed her. Its tentacles twisted ever so softly in the deep, dark water.

Up and down the fabric moved. Curling and uncurling. In short, the curtains freaked Simone out.

There was nothing she could do about it except lie back down on the mountain of pillows and try to sleep.

Later that night, Simone woke up with a start. She sat up in bed. She had dreamed that something soft was touching her face.

Simone stared at the wispy white curtains.

Moonlight was sifting through the window. Just like every other night, the curtains were performing their strange, watery dance in the breeze. Curling up and down, they reached into the room. *A snow-coloured octopus*, thought Simone. White tentacles drifting through a dark, giant pool. A pool filled with drowned flowers and hummingbirds. Now and then the breeze would shift, and the tentacles seemed to reach for the bed.

Fred meowed. "It's all right," said Simone, petting the kitten. "Go back to sleep." By comforting the kitten, Simone felt a rush of courage. Fred meowed again as the sound whispered through the room, but the girl was soon asleep.

In the morning, Simone woke up full of energy. The room was bright with sunlight and the curtains were still. She could smell the delicious aroma of homemade breakfast. Simone pulled on her dressing gown and quickly joined her great-aunt in the kitchen.

"Hope you slept well, honey," said Aunt Glory, pouring a glass of orange juice for the girl.

"Yes, thanks," mumbled Simone. "It was just a little cool with the windows open."

"Well, that's funny," said Aunt Glory with a frown. "Because last night I thought I'd try it your way."

"What do you mean?" Simone asked.

The old woman stirred a pan on the hob. "I heard on the TV last night that it might get cold," she said. "So I went in while you were asleep and shut the windows. They were closed all night long."

Her great-aunt added: "By the way, where's that precious little kitten of yours?"

Simone froze. She hadn't seen Fred all morning. He should have followed her into the kitchen. The girl ran back to her bedroom. She couldn't see Fred sleeping there, as she had hoped. When she had woken up, she threw aside the covers to hop out. Fred couldn't still be trapped under there, could he?

Simone straightened the sheets, but Fred was not there. Instead, Simone saw claw marks, ripping the blanket. The marks made straight, even lines running towards the window. It was as if the kitten had been pulled in that direction. Pulled by something that was able to reach inside the room with a long, long arm.

ABOUT THE AUTHOR

Michael Dahl, the author of the Library of Doom
and Troll Hunters series, is an expert on fear. He is
afraid of heights (but he still flies). He is afraid of
small, enclosed spaces (but his house is crammed
with over 3000 books). He is afraid of ghosts (but
that same house is haunted). He hopes that by
writing about fear, he will eventually be able to
overcome his own. So far it is not working. But he
is afraid to stop. He claims that, if he had to, he
would travel to Mount Doom in order to throw in
a dangerous piece of jewellery. Even though he is
afraid of volcanoes. And jewellery.

ABOUT THE ILLUSTRATOR

Xavier Bonet is an illustrator and comic-book artist who resides in Barcelona. Experienced in 2D illustration, he has worked as an animator and a background artist for several different production companies. He aims to create works full of colour, texture and sensation, using both traditional and digital tools. His work in children's literature is inspired by magic and fantasy as well as his passion for art.

MICHAEL DAHL TELLS ALL

William Shakespeare, my favourite non-scary-story writer, once asked, "Where is Fancy bred?" That was his way of saying how does our imagination (our "Fancy") come up with its ideas? Even he wasn't sure. Shakespeare was, however, inspired by his friends, by books and poems he had read and by plays he had seen. Same for me, though I've seen more TV and films than plays. On the following pages, I've tried to recall where I got the ideas for the stories in this book.

THE DARKEST BRIDGE

Can we all agree that bridges are just plain scary?
I've always been afraid of them. Recently I read a
book about "crybaby bridges". These are supposedly
haunted bridges, the sites of tragic car accidents
where, as a result, the spirits of the dead can still be
heard crying at night. Sounds like a story to me!

THE WAITING POOL

I had a paddling pool as a child, and my friends and I
enjoyed many hours playing in it during the summer.
One of my favourite things to do as an author is to
take something seemingly innocent, like a child's
pool, and turn it into something terrifying. I was
also thinking of the legendary "Fountain of Youth",
a pool that magically washes away the years of older
people who swim in it or drink its water. Well, what
if I combined those two things, and then twisted it?
What if the water made you really, really old?

BIG FURRY

The cellar in this story is based on several different basements I've been in, including the one in my aunt's old place that used to be a boarding house for loggers in the middle of northern Minnesota, USA. My aunt had a black fur coat that hung on a hook just inside the basement door. No matter how many times I'd seen it before, that furry mass always looked like a monster to me. Or one of the hungry black bears that roam the snowy woods of Minnesota.

A HAND IN THE DARK

I'm a big fan of old science fiction movies. I watched them as a child, and I particularly liked the ones where a science experiment goes wrong and creates a monster. The creepiest monsters are the ones that look like goo or tar. They ooze under doors and drip down stairs to attack their victims. I figured a good place for a monster to attack would be one of those eerily isolated cinema screens at the end of a super-long corridor. Because if you did hear something strange, you'd think it was coming from the screen, right? Not from the creature sitting next to you. (This is one reason I never go to the cinema alone!)

FLUSHED

All those poor, dead goldfish. They don't even get a decent garden burial like a cat or a dog. Just a flush! Here's another story where I turned a normal, everyday event on its head. Besides, wouldn't a huge goldfish look intimidating?

THE HORNLOCK

This little tale has such a spooky origin that I can't even tell you the whole story. Just know that a friend of mine, when she was young, had an imaginary friend who may not have been so . . . imaginary. That imaginary friend's name was very similar to Hornlock. Secondly, my brother-in-law, Larry, used to sleep out on the porch in the summer as a child, and he very often had nightmares out there, all alone. I smooshed those ideas together to create this story. Whenever I re-read it, it still gives me shivers.

THE NIGHT OCTOPUS

One of the coolest things your imagination does is make you see two things at the same time. You look at a strange shape in the bark of a tree and you see a face. You look at a small cloud and see a flying saucer. Or you look at curtains waving in the wind, as I did as a small child, and you see them as a living creature . . . with tentacles.

GLOSSARY

absorbing taking something in, or sucking or swallowing it up

aroma smell that is usually pleasant

howl make a loud noise that sounds like a dog or a wolf

limp walk with difficulty, usually because of an injury

plunge fall steeply or sharply

ravine steep, narrow valley

substance physical matter of which someone or something is made

temperature degree of heat or cold in something, usually measured by a thermometer

tentacles long, flexible limbs of some animals, such as an octopus and a squid

threatening giving signs or warning of something

vibration trembling motion

wispy feathery

DISCUSSION QUESTIONS

1. When Larry meets a monster in "The Hornlock", he isn't sure whether it's a dream. Talk about a time when you were unable to tell the difference between what was a dream and what was real life.

2. In "The Night Octopus", what is the connection between the curtains in the guest bedroom and Simone's kitten, Fred? Discuss the possibilities.

3. Can you explain why the goldfish in "Flushed" describe Rachel as having "sad, sad eyes"? What details in the text support your explanation?

WRITING PROMPTS

1. Describe the main characters in "The Darkest Bridge" in a few sentences. Which details from the story support your descriptions of these characters?

2. Write a version of the story "A Hand in the Dark" from Angus's point of view. How is his experience different from Jasmine's?

3. I was inspired to write "Big Furry" by some spooky basements I have seen in my life. Think of a place that gives you the chills. Then write a story based on it!

MICHAEL DAHL'S

REALLY SCARY STORIES